# CONTENTS

# CHAPTER 1

# A FIELD TRIP

Hakeem Bennett carefully climbed up the highest peak of the Adirondack Mountains. He relied only on his fingers and toes to find the little cracks in the rock. The small spaces would allow him to scale the summit. No ropes or safety harnesses for Hakeem Bennett! It was just him . . .

"Hakeem!"

. . . Just him, Hakeem Bennett, alone against the mountain. Of course, since he was also a famous geologist, Hakeem had professional responsibilities.

# SUPER DC HEROES

# SUPERMAN

# THE KID WHO SAVED SUPERMAN

WRITTEN BY
PAUL KUPPERBERG

ILLUSTRATED BY
MIN SUNG KU AND
LEE LOUGHRIDGE

SUPERMAN CREATED BY
JERRY SIEGEL AND
JOE SHUSTER

**www.raintreepublishers.co.uk**
Visit our website to find out
more information about
Raintree books.

Phone 0845 6044371
Fax +44 (0) 1865 312263
Email myorders@capstonepub.co.uk

Customers from outside the UK please telephone +44 1865 312262

Raintree is an imprint of Capstone Global Library Limited,
a company incorporated in England and Wales having its registered office at
7 Pilgrim Street, London, EC4V 6LB – Registered company number: 6695582

"Raintree" is a registered trademark of Pearson Education Limited, under licence to
Capstone Global Library Limited

First published by Stone Arch Books in 2010
First published in hardback in the United Kingdom in 2010
Paperback edition first published in the United Kingdom in 2010
The moral rights of the proprietor have been asserted.

Art Director: Bob Lentz
Designer: Brann Garvey
UK Editor: Vaarunika Dharmapala
Originated by Capstone Global Library Ltd
Printed and bound in China by Leo Paper Products Ltd

Photos courtesy of Nathanael Greene School, Brooklyn, New York, USA

ISBN 978 1 406214 96 3 (hardback)
14 13 12 11 10
10 9 8 7 6 5 4 3 2 1

ISBN 978 1 406215 10 6 (paperback)
14 13 12 11 10
10 9 8 7 6 5 4 3 2 1

**British Library Cataloguing in Publication Data**
A full catalogue record for this book is available from the British Library.

Hakeem would stop along the way to the top of the world and collect rock samples. He tucked them in his rucksack for later examination.

"Hakeem Bennett!" shouted the head teacher, Ms Schneider, from far behind him. "You're daydreaming again! We're stopping for lunch."

"Huh?" replied Hakeem with a shake of his head. He hadn't been paying attention. Johanna Schneider, the school's nature expert, had been telling the class about the animals, insects, and rocks that could be found in the Adirondack Mountains. Once again, Hakeem had become lost in his own fantasies.

"Yes, Ms Schneider," said Hakeem. His cheeks burned with embarrassment at the sound of his classmates' laughter.

Hakeem wasn't a geologist. He was just a boy who had wandered ahead of the rest of his science class. They were on a field trip from the Nathanael Greene School in Brooklyn, New York.

Geology was one of Hakeem's favourite subjects. He hoped to be a geologist one day. If he ever wanted that day to come, though, he had to start paying closer attention to the real world. Hakeem rejoined his classmates. They gathered around their teacher, Mr Brown, and pulled off their rucksacks.

"After we eat," said Mr Brown, "we'll continue up the trail. It leads to the largest marble cave entrance in North America."

Although he was visually impaired, Mr Brown – with help from his dog, Stanley – knew the mountains better than anyone.

Hakeem couldn't wait to explore the mountain's marble caves. Unlike the other kids, he didn't believe stories about the caves being haunted by the ghosts of old miners. Even without ghosts, the caves were interesting enough. A real geologist could study all sorts of rocks and learn a lot about how the world was formed.

Once Ms Schneider and Mr Brown were sure the class had cleaned up their rubbish, they all continued on their way. Soon, the class rounded a bend in the trail. There, behind some trees, were the giant twin entrances to the Great Caves. Every pupil oohed and aahed at the sight.

Hakeem stared into the mouth of the larger cave. Ms Schneider explained how the giant network of caves had been carved inside the mountain.

"Many caves are made up of limestone, but the Adirondack Mountains have caves made of marble," explained the head teacher. "Marble is an extremely hard rock. Over many years, however, water can get into the cracks of the marble and start to dissolve the rock, making the cracks bigger and bigger."

"Believe it or not," added Mr Brown, "those tiny cracks eventually became these tunnels and caves. Thousands of years ago, flood waters rushed through the valleys between these mountains, carving the caves out of the marble. Does anyone know what happened next?"

"I do," said Hakeem, raising his hand.

Mr Brown was glad that Hakeem was participating instead of daydreaming. "Yes, Hakeem?" he said.

"Something, like a change in the climate or an earthquake, made the water drain from the valleys," said Hakeem. "The water also drained out of the caves, so now we can go inside them."

"That's right," said Mr Brown. "And as soon as we review the safety regulations, that's exactly what we're going to do!"

# CHAPTER 2

# EARTHQUAKE!

Thousands of miles away, a blue and red streak sped through the sky – it was Superman! Below him, the mountains rumbled like thunder. An earthquake was shuddering through the area!

Hovering in the sky, Superman used his super-vision to see if anyone needed his help. As powerful as he was, not even Superman could stop an earthquake, which shook the Earth's crust deep underground. He knew that even a minor earthquake could be extremely dangerous.

Superman was following a string of earthquakes as they rippled their way around the world. The Man of Steel did his best to help those in danger's way.

Superman's super-hearing picked up a sudden, distant rumble. He turned in mid-air and saw that a layer of snow atop a high peak was sliding down the mountainside. In a valley below the rushing wall of snow sat a small village.

"Great Krypton!" Superman exclaimed. "The whole town will be buried!"

Superman sped towards the great mound of sliding snow. The Man of Steel knew he couldn't stop all of the snow at once. Instead, he flew back and forth beneath it, blasting the icy tidal wave with his heat vision.

In an instant, the air beneath the avalanche boiled. The snow quickly melted and turned into steam!

*That was close,* Superman thought as he flew away.

With his X-ray vision, the Man of Steel peered deep into the ground beneath the mountains. A fresh crack in the rock below the ground was spreading westwards, from France and the European continent out into the Atlantic Ocean.

"At the rate this series of earthquakes is moving, it will cross the ocean in no time," said Superman. "It's on a straight line for the United States – and New York!"

In a flash, the Man of Steel was gone.

Back in the Adirondack Mountains, Hakeem was waiting for his class to enter the marble caves. Ms Schneider and Mr Brown were repeating the safety information and handing out torches to everyone. Hakeem had already received his torch. Now he had to wait, and he was getting bored.

When Hakeem was bored, his mind began to wander. As he stood by the smaller of the two cave entrances, Hakeem imagined exploring for a treasure hidden deep inside the Adirondack Mountains.

Hakeem poked his head into the cave. The entrance was so big, there was hardly any difference between the inside and outside of the cave. Keeping his hand on the cave wall, Hakeem took another step inside. Still no change.

Hakeem took another step and then a few more, and, all of a sudden, he felt the difference. There was a cool, damp feel to the air. Hakeem had gone just a step deeper than the rays of the sun could fully reach.

"I'm spelunking!" Hakeem whispered to himself, using the word he'd seen in a geology book.

What treasure was he searching for? The lost gold of Mountain Man Joe, of course!

Hakeem's dad had told him the legend of the old miner. Joe had lived alone in the Adirondack Mountains more than a hundred years ago. He was famous for making friends with the native people and for hunting the biggest and meanest beasts in the forests. There was even a story about Mountain Man Joe wrestling a giant grizzly bear for a fortune in gold.

Mountain Man Joe won the fight, but he didn't need the riches. He hid the gold in the mountains. It had never been found.

Hakeem thought about a great oak chest bursting with gold coins. *Whoever finds it will be rich!* he thought. *What would I do with that fortune?*

Without thinking, Hakeem switched on his torch and walked deeper into the darkening cave. He knew he shouldn't be going any farther, but it wasn't really a big deal yet. All Hakeem had to do was turn his head, and he could still see light from the cave's entrance.

Besides, Hakeem was serious about geology. Maybe he hadn't been inside a cave before, but he had read many books about them. Hakeem almost considered himself an expert explorer!

**R**UMMMMMMMMBLE!

Then the ground beneath Hakeem's feet began to tremble. Boulders started to tumble all around him. Hakeem suddenly realized just how little he really knew about caves!

# CHAPTER 3

# LOST IN THE CAVERNS

"Everybody come close to us!" shouted Ms Schneider.

The children quickly gathered around their teachers. The ground started to roll under their feet, rumbling like a dozen speeding trains. They were all frightened.

Ms Schneider and Mr Brown were grateful they had not gone into the caves, yet. Even from where they stood, they could hear the sounds of large rocks and boulders crashing to the ground.

"Is everybody here?" asked Mr Brown.

*Ruff! Ruff!* Mr Brown's dog stood near the entrance of the small cave, barking loudly.

"Something's wrong with Stanley," said Mr Brown.

Ms Schneider looked over at the mouth of the cave. She thought she saw a quick flash of a green shirt. Then, with a crash that made her bones shudder, the side of the mountain collapsed and covered the entrance to both caves. SMASH!

"Hakeem!" cried Ms Schneider.

In the sky above, Superman heard her frightened shout. It took him only a moment to locate the trouble with his super-vision and fly towards the caves.

"Is everybody all right?" Superman asked, landing near the class.

"Superman!" said Ms Schneider. "Thank goodness you're here! One of our pupils is missing. I think he went inside the small cave before it collapsed."

The Man of Steel narrowed his eyes. He used his X-ray vision to look through the pile of rocks blocking the cave entrance.

"I see him," Superman said. "He hasn't been hurt. I'll have him out of there in a few minutes."

Inside the cave, Hakeem coughed and sneezed from the dust and dirt swirling in the air. If not for the small torch he held, it would have been too dark to see inside the collapsed cave.

"Hello?" Hakeem called out.

No answer. He only heard the echo of his own voice.

"There has to be another way out of here," Hakeem whispered to himself. He thought maybe if he kept talking out loud, he wouldn't be so frightened.

"I'll head this way," he said, taking a few slow, careful steps into the darkness.

The ground began to shake again. "It's just an aftershock. Small tremors that come after the big earthquake," Hakeem said.

The little tremors grew bigger. Hakeem felt like he was standing on a runaway skateboard instead of solid ground.

Moments later, Hakeem realized that he *wasn't* standing on solid ground anymore. The ground felt thinner than an eggshell. Then Hakeem heard a sound that sent tingles up his spine.

Hakeem stopped in terror. "If I just move slowly, I'll be okay," he said to himself.

Trying to be as light as possible, Hakeem propped up on to his tiptoes. He started to walk, slowly and carefully, across the crackling ground.

"Maybe not!" Hakeem screamed. He looked down. The ground beneath his feet was cracking like a sheet of ice.

With no other choice, Hakeem started running. He quickly scrambled across the crumbling ground, hoping to find a solid spot. It was no use. With a frightful roar, the ground split open. Suddenly, Hakeem was falling, head over heels, into the darkness.

Outside the caves, the same quake shook the earth. Trees toppled and rocks and boulders tumbled off the peaks of the Adirondack Mountains. Superman stood in front of the science class, shielding them from harm with his super-strong body.

When the earthquake finally ended, Superman spoke with Ms Schneider and Mr Brown. "You and the children will be safer if you head back down the trail to your bus," he said.

"What about Hakeem?" asked Ms Schneider. "He's still trapped in there!"

"I'll get him out," Superman promised.

When the students and teachers had disappeared down the trail, the Man of Steel began digging through the mass of rocks blocking the cave entrance.

"I have to be very careful," Superman reminded himself. "Digging too quickly could cause the cave to collapse even more. Hakeem could be injured by the falling rocks . . . or worse."

Superman used his X-ray vision to check if Hakeem was still okay. As the rocks faded from his view, the inside of the cave looked empty. Hakeem was gone!

Superman quickly backed away. He flew with all of his might at the wall of rock blocking the cave entrance.

**WHAM!** He burst through the rocks like a pebble through wet tissue.

"Help!" cried a voice from far away.

"Hakeem!" shouted Superman. He scanned the cave and saw a gaping hole in the ground.

"Help me!" came the voice again. This time, it sounded even farther away.

In a single bound, the Man of Steel jumped into the hole. "Don't worry, Hakeem," Superman called into the darkness. "I'm on my way!"

# CHAPTER 4

# A DEADLY GREEN LIGHT

**SPLASH!** Hakeem sputtered and coughed. The cold, rushing waters of an underground river swept him deeper into the cave. His arms flailed wildly, reaching for something to grab.

"Help!" he cried out.

When the cave floor split open, Hakeem had fallen into the frigid water. The river rushed along and spilled through a hole in the cave wall. It poured out into a large underground pool, carrying Hakeem like a leaf caught in a storm.

"Help me, please!" Hakeem cried again. Then the water dragged him under.

Gasping for breath, pumping his arms with all his strength, Hakeem popped to the surface. He quickly swam to the shore.

Hakeem climbed on to the ledge and stood for a moment. Amazingly, he had not been injured during the plunge through the rushing waters. He still held tight to the torch, and it still worked.

"I'll find a way out," he told himself softly. "I have to."

As Hakeem looked around, he spotted a green glow in the distance. He pointed the torch towards it, but the beam was not powerful enough to reach the glow. Hakeem moved closer until the circle of light fell on a strange green rock.

"Emeralds don't glow like that," Hakeem said to himself. "It looks more like a space rock or some kind of meteor."

"Hakeem!" a deep voice suddenly called from the darkness.

Hakeem whirled around. "Hello?!" he shouted. "Is somebody there?"

"Hold on, Hakeem," said the voice. "I'm going to get you out of there."

## WHOOOOSH!

From out of the shadows soared a man in a blue uniform and red cape.

"Superman!" Hakeem said in relief.

"Are you okay, Hakeem?" asked the Man of Steel.

"Yes," replied Hakeem, "now that you're here!"

"I'm glad you're all right," said the Man of Steel. He landed on a rocky ledge and held out a hand to Hakeem. "Now, let's get out of here and . . . and . . . "

Superman's voice suddenly grew weak. "What's wrong . . . with me . . . ?" he wondered aloud.

"Superman?" Hakeem said, his eyes growing wide with fear.

"We . . . we better get out of . . . of here," Superman started to say. Then he groaned in pain and collapsed on to the ground.

"Superman!" Hakeem yelled. He ran to the Man of Steel's side. "Please! You've got to get up!"

The super hero could only groan in pain. Hakeem didn't know what was wrong.

"You're Superman!" Hakeem exclaimed. "Nothing's supposed to hurt you!"

Still, something was hurting the Man of Steel, but Hakeem could not have known. He had never met a real super hero before. While some of his friends were big fans of Superman and other heroes, Hakeem had always been more interested in geology, science, and rocks.

"If only this had something to do with rocks, maybe I'd know what to do," Hakeem said.

"R-rock . . . " Superman whispered.

Hakeem looked around in desperation. How were they supposed to get out of here if even Superman was helpless? Then the light from his torch flickered and dimmed. Hakeem swallowed hard.

*The battery is probably running out,* he thought. *Soon, it'll go dead, and we'll be in the dark.*

*No,* Hakeem reminded himself. *It won't be completely dark.* The glowing rock gave off light. He could see the green glow reflected on Superman's face.

"Green . . . rock . . . " Superman said, his voice growing weaker.

"Yes, Superman," Hakeem said. "A green rock. I don't know what kind. Maybe it's a meteor or something."

Superman's fingers grasped Hakeem's arm. The boy turned to look at the Man of Steel. When light from his torch fell on the super hero's face, Hakeem gasped.

"Superman!" Hakeem yelled. "Your skin is turning green!"

Just then, Hakeem remembered.

"That's it!" he exclaimed. "It's a meteor. I've read about this type of radioactive rock before. It's kryptonite – the only thing in the universe that can hurt Superman!"

# CHAPTER 5

# A SUPER RESCUE

Hakeem Bennett raced towards the kryptonite. He remembered that the green rock came from Superman's home planet, Krypton. When Krypton exploded, pieces of the planet turned radioactive, giving off dangerous energy. Hakeem knew that the energy was harmful only to people born on Krypton, like Superman.

If he did not get the super hero away from the kryptonite, the Man of Steel would die. Hakeem would be trapped in the cave forever!

The boulder of kryptonite was ten feet from the rocky ledge and the pool of water that Hakeem had fallen into. Even if the boy could find a safe place for Superman, the Man of Steel was too heavy to move.

"What blocks radiation?" Hakeem wondered aloud. He paused for a moment, trying to remember what he had read in science textbooks. "Lead!" he suddenly recalled. "Dentists use lead aprons to protect their patients from X-rays. But where am I supposed to find lead?"

Hakeem's torch flickered and dimmed even more. He had only a few minutes until the battery died, and he would be in the dark.

From somewhere deep below his feet, Hakeem heard a deep rumbling sound, like the roar of an approaching train.

Hakeem felt another earthquake and heard water splashing around him.

"Water!" he cried out. "Water blocks radiation! Maybe this pool is deep enough!"

The rocky ledge began to shake. The glowing kryptonite boulder trembled and rocked in place. It was too heavy for Hakeem to move on his own, but maybe the earthquake would help.

Hakeem threw all his weight into the rocking boulder. "Oof!" he cried out. The green boulder didn't budge.

*Again!* Hakeem thought, backing up and taking another run at the radioactive rock.

WHAM! He slammed into the boulder.

"Ow!" the boy shouted in pain.

As Hakeem grabbed his aching shoulder, he saw the chunk of kryptonite wobble. Then another earthquake shook the ground, and the boulder tumbled forwards.

**CRAAAAACK!** The ledge beneath Hakeem's feet suddenly split in two. The kryptonite tilted towards the water.

Hakeem quickly jumped away from the green rock. The kryptonite tumbled into the water. **Splash!**

Hakeem stood on the shaking ledge. Rocks and chunks of stone fell all around him. At that moment, his torch flickered one last time and went dark.

"Superman!" he yelled. "Are you okay?"

A strong hand grasped Hakeem's arm in the dark.

"I'm right here, Hakeem," said Superman, stepping out of the darkness. "And I'm just fine, thanks to you. Now, hold tight! I'll have us out of here in a flash!"

Superman scooped Hakeem into his arms and flew him through the darkened tunnels towards the entrance of the cave.

By the time they landed in the clearing outside the marble cave, the quake had ended. Hakeem was still shaking.

"Thank you for saving me from the kryptonite," Superman said. "It's a good thing you know so much about science."

"I've always liked geology," Hakeem told the Man of Steel. "I studied quakes and how they're caused when two parts of the earth's crust rub against each other."

Superman stared towards the ground. "That's right," he said. "It happens along cracks in the crust called fault lines. My X-ray vision shows me there's a fault line under these mountains."

"If only there was a way to stop the two parts from rubbing together," Hakeem said.

"There is," said the Man of Steel. "It's a big job . . . even for Superman!"

Hakeem grinned. "Wow! You mean, I worked it out before you did?"

"That's right, Hakeem," said Superman. "And if you hadn't got rid of the kryptonite, we'd still be trapped down inside the cave. Now, let's get you back to your class, and then I'll take care of that underground problem of ours."

Superman and Hakeem walked down the nature trail towards the bus. "The rest of the kids aren't going to believe what happened," Hakeem said.

"Well, maybe they'll believe me," said Superman.

"In fact," Superman continued, "I think you'll soon be known as the kid who saved Superman!"

"Do you really think so?" said Hakeem.

"I do," replied Superman.

"I still would've liked to bring something back to show the class," Hakeem said. "Maybe a piece of that hidden treasure."

"I didn't think a scientist like you would believe in the legend of Mountain Man Joe," said Superman.

Hakeem looked up at the Man of Steel and smiled. "After a day like today," he said, "Nothing would surprise me."

FROM THE DESK OF CLARK KENT

# THE KID WHO SAVED SUPERMAN

Thirteen-year-old Hakeem Bennett is the real-life Kid Who Saved Superman. The Year Nine pupil at the Nathanael Greene School in Brooklyn, New York, won a national writing contest to be named the saviour of the Man of Steel.

His winning entry was chosen from hundreds of other contestants who wrote about a real hero at their school, describing what makes that person a hero in their opinion. Congratulations, Hakeem!

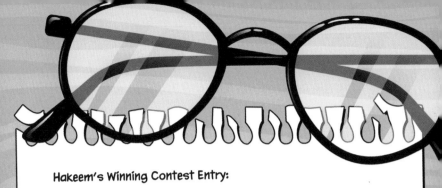

**Hakeem's Winning Contest Entry:**

My teacher Mr Brown is visually impaired. That's not what makes him a hero. It is because he takes public transportation everyday with Stanley his dog to school. That is why he is a true, everyday super hero.

In our class we had a project of being blindfolded and trying to find our way around the class. It was hard for me. In our school it is hard. Being in special education, we learn to recognize our disabilities.

Mr Brown doesn't want to take access-a-ride to work being driven from his house to work. I feel sad he can't see the beautiful things around. That bothers me. To ride the train to East New York in Brooklyn is chaotic and not the safest even for people who do not have a disability. The travelling in the snow and ice with Stanley makes him even more courageous.

Mr Brown is my pick for our school super hero. He could serve as a super hero for all.

# BIOGRAPHIES

**Paul Kupperberg** has written many books for children, like *Wishbone: The Sirian Conspiracy*, and *Powerpuff Girls: Buttercup's Terrible Temper Tantrums*. He has also written over 600 comic book stories about Superman, Spider-Man, Hulk, Scooby Doo, and many others. Paul's own character creations include Arion: Lord of Atlantis, Checkmate, and Takion. He has also been an editor for DC Comics, Weekly World News, and World Wrestling Entertainment. Paul lives with his wife, Robin, son, Max, and dog, Spike.

**Min Sung Ku** dreamed of becoming a comic book illustrator as a child. When he was only six years old, he drew a picture of Superman standing behind the American flag. He has since achieved his childhood dream, having illustrated popular comics such as the Justice League, Batman, Spider-Man, Krpyto the Superdog, and, of course, Superman himself. Min lives with his lovely wife and their beautiful twin daughters, Elisia and Eliana.

**Lee Loughridge** has been working in comics for more than 14 years. He currently lives in a tent on the beach.

# GLOSSARY

**examination**  careful inspection

**fault**  large crack in the earth's surface that can cause earthquakes

**geology**  study of earth's layers of soil and rock

**legend**  story handed down from long ago

**marble**  hard stone, often used for buildings and sculptures

**radioactive**  materials that give off harmful energy

**spelunking**  exploring caves

**summit**  highest point, such as the top of a mountain

**tremor**  shaking or trembling movement, often caused by earthquakes

**visually impaired**  having greatly reduced vision or sight

# DISCUSSION QUESTIONS

1. In the story, Hakeem's favourite subject is geology, the study of earth's layers of soil and rock. What's your favourite subject? Why do you like it?

2. What do you think would have happened to Superman if Hakeem hadn't saved him? Would the Man of Steel have escaped alive? Explain your answer.

3. In real life, Hakeem Bennett's hero is his teacher, Mr Brown. Who is your real-life hero?

# WRITING PROMPTS

1. Write a second part to this story. Does Superman fix the fault lines? Will he find the treasure? You decide.

2. Imagine you had to save the Man of Steel. How would your talents and abilities help save Superman? Write a story about it.

3. In this story, Hakeem had heard of the legend of Mountain Man Joe. Have you ever heard a legend or a ghost story? Write about it, or make one up.